The Pet Keeper Fairies

For Leandro D'Olivera with my love

Special thanks to
Sue Mongredien

ORCHARD BOOKS
338 Euston Road, London NW1 3BH
Orchard Books Australia
Level 17/207 Kent Street, Sydney, NSW 2000
A Paperback Original

First published in Great Britain in 2006

© 2008 Rainbow Magic Limited.
A HIT Entertainment company. Rainbow Magic
is a trademark of Rainbow Magic Limited.
Reg. U.S. Pat. & Tm. Off. And other countries.

HiT entertainment

Illustrations © Georgie Ripper 2006

A CIP catalogue record for this book is available
from the British Library.

ISBN 978 1 84616 167 4
9 10 8

Printed in Great Britain

Orchard Books is a division of Hachette Children's Books,
an Hachette Livre UK company

www.hachettelivre.co.uk

Harriet
the Hamster
Fairy

by Daisy Meadows

illustrated by Georgie Ripper

ORCHARD BOOKS

www.rainbowmagic.co.uk

Fairies with their pets I see
And yet no pet has chosen me!
So I will get some of my own
To share my perfect frosty home.

This spell I cast. Its aim is clear:
To bring the magic pets straight here.
Pet Keeper Fairies soon will see
Their seven pets living with me!

Contents

Hamster-sitting

"Here we go," Kirsty Tate said to her best friend, Rachel Walker, turning the key in the back door of her neighbours' house. "Nibbles! Time for breakfast!" she called, as the door swung open. "Just wait until you see him," she said to Rachel with a grin. "He's adorable. I love hamster-sitting!"

Kirsty's neighbour, Jamie Cooper, had asked Kirsty to feed Nibbles, his little orange and white hamster, while he and his parents were away. She had said yes immediately.

"We just need to top up his food and water," Kirsty told Rachel. "And if we're lucky, he might eat his sunflower seeds out of our hands!"

"How sweet!" Rachel said. "Where's his cage?"

"Over here," Kirsty replied, heading into the lounge.

An excited feeling bubbled up inside Rachel as she followed her friend. This was another pet that they were going to see, after all, and over the last few days, she and Kirsty had had some very exciting pet adventures!

Rachel was staying with Kirsty's family for a whole week, and on the very first day of her holiday, the two girls had met the Pet Keeper Fairies of Fairyland! The fairies had asked Rachel and Kirsty for their help. Jack Frost had wanted a pet of his own, but in Fairyland, pets choose their owners and none of them had chosen Jack Frost. He had been so annoyed by this that he had stolen the Pet Keeper Fairies' magical pets for himself! Luckily, the pets had all escaped from Jack Frost into the human world, but that meant that now they were wandering around lost!

Rachel and Kirsty were helping the Pet Keeper Fairies find the magic pets before Jack Frost's mean goblin servants did. So far, the girls had found four: Shimmer the kitten, Misty the bunny, Sparky the guinea pig and Sunny the puppy. But there were still three pets missing.

Kirsty led Rachel across the lounge to the side table where Nibbles' cage stood. But when the girls arrived, they saw at once that something was wrong: the cage door was wide open!

"Oh, no!" Kirsty cried. "Don't tell me that Nibbles has managed to escape on

my very first day of looking after him!"
She carefully put her hand into the
cage and searched through the wood
shavings and newspaper shreds for the
little hamster, but it was too late. The
cage was empty.

She and Rachel began searching
everywhere they could think of in the
lounge. They looked under the table,
around all the chairs and behind the
television. But there was no sign
of Jamie's hamster.

"Nibbles!" Rachel
called, picking up
his food bowl
and rattling it.
"Nibbles, come
and have
something to eat."

"Jamie's going to
be so upset if he comes home and
Nibbles is missing," Kirsty said,
anxiously. "Nibbles! Where are you?"

"He could be absolutely anywhere in
the house," Rachel said. "Come on,
let's try another room."

Kirsty nodded and the girls headed
out of the lounge. But just as they
reached the door, Kirsty spotted
something. "Rachel, look!" she cried,
bending down to examine the carpet.

She picked up a stray wood shaving
and held it up triumphantly. "A clue!"

"It must have been stuck to one
of Nibbles' feet when he climbed out
of the cage," Rachel guessed. "Look,
there's another by the doorway.
And another!"

The two girls followed the trail of
wood shavings out into the hall and
began searching around the coat rack
and the telephone table.

Kirsty picked up the
morning post from
the doormat and
noticed that some
of the envelopes
were a little
shredded. "Look!"
she exclaimed.
"Someone's been
tearing the post!"
Then she smiled as
she realised what had
happened. "Hamsters shred
paper to make nests, don't they?" she
added. "I think Nibbles must have
started trying to make a nest here!" She
giggled as she put the letters on the
table, safely out of reach. "Where did
he go next, I wonder?"

"This way," Rachel said, spotting
a couple of pieces of shredded paper
near the kitchen. "Come on!"

In the kitchen, the girls peered under
the table and chairs, but there was no
sign of a small, furry hamster.

"Someone's been nibbling this fruit,"
Kirsty said, picking up
an apple from the fruit
bowl. Tiny teeth had
punctured the skin
in several places.

"Nibbles must
have stopped for
a snack." Then she
frowned. "How on
earth did he get up
onto the kitchen
counter, though?"

Rachel pointed at the nearby curtain. "Hamsters have strong claws," she pointed out. "I expect Nibbles climbed up the curtain to reach the counter top." She grinned, imagining the scene. "Nibbles is very clever, isn't he?"

"Yes," Kirsty agreed, scanning the kitchen and the curtains, hoping to spot a flash of orange and white fur. "But he's not here any more. We'd better keep looking."

Rachel suddenly froze on the spot. "Sssh!" she whispered to Kirsty, putting a finger to her lips. "What's that noise?"

Both girls stood still and listened
hard. They could just hear a faint
scratching sound coming from
the hallway.

Kirsty grinned at Rachel. "Phew! It
must be Nibbles scratching," she said.
"All we need to do is follow that
sound, and it should lead us straight
to one very adventurous hamster!"

The girls tiptoed out
of the kitchen in the
direction of the
scratching noise.
The sound
seemed to be
getting louder as
they approached
the cupboard
under the stairs.

"Nibbles, I'm coming to get you!" Kirsty giggled. She stepped forwards to open the cupboard door, but before she could quite reach it, the door swung open by itself – and out jumped one of Jack Frost's horrible green goblins!

Harriet Drops In

"Oh!" gasped Kirsty, as the goblin laughed rudely, charged out of the cupboard and ran up the stairs.

Before either girl could say a word, a second goblin stuck his head over the banisters and cheekily blew raspberries at them!

Kirsty and Rachel looked at each other.

Goblins in the Coopers' house could mean only one thing!

"There must be a fairy pet nearby," Rachel whispered, her heart thumping.

"Yes, and we've got to find it before the goblins do!" Kirsty agreed, her eyes darting everywhere.

"Go away!" came a rude shout from upstairs.

Rachel and Kirsty both looked up to
see that there were now three goblins
peering over the banisters.

"We won't go away," Kirsty said,
putting her hands on her hips. "We've
come to feed Jamie's hamster. We're
supposed to be here!"

The goblins all burst out laughing.
"Hamster gone missing, has he?"
one of them managed to say
between sniggers.

"Guess what? We let it out!" another one guffawed.

"What did you do that for?" Kirsty asked crossly.

"To make the pesky fairy pet hamster come to the rescue, of course," the third goblin replied slyly. "And when it does, we'll catch it and take it back to Jack Frost!"

Rachel frowned. "So you've set a trap for the magic hamster?" she asked. "How horrible!"

"Well, if the fairy hamster does come, we'll find it first," Kirsty said, a determined look on her face. "And we'll give it back to Harriet the Hamster Fairy!"

"No chance," shouted the first goblin. And then all three goblins disappeared, and the girls heard their big goblin feet thundering up another flight of stairs.

Kirsty groaned. "This house is so big; it's got three storeys and an attic! How are we ever going to find two little hamsters before those sneaky goblins do?"

"If there are two hamsters," Rachel reminded her. "The magic hamster might not have come to Nibbles' rescue yet."

Out of the corner of her eye, Kirsty suddenly caught a glimpse of sparkling red light in the lounge.

Curiously, she pushed the door open to
see what was happening inside. "I think
the magic hamster is here, Rachel," she
said, her eyes wide as she gazed at the
Coopers' lounge.

Both girls stood in the doorway,
staring at the transformation of the
room before them. The woollen rug
had become a heap of wood shavings
and shredded newspaper. Hamster toys
were scattered everywhere, together

with a mini-maze and two large
running wheels. There were even bowls
of nuts and seeds standing on the floor.

"Just look!" Kirsty said. "This is
hamster heaven!"

Rachel nodded. "This is definitely pet
fairy magic in action," she said with
a grin.

"So we'd better find the magic
hamster," Kirsty pointed out, "before
the goblins do!"

Rachel peeped into the mini-maze. "With a bit of luck, Nibbles will be attracted to this hamster heaven, and come scuttling in here any second," she said. "I mean, what hamster could resist all this?" As she turned to look around, her gaze fell upon the sofa and she bit her lip in excitement. "Kirsty," she said quietly, so as not to scare the little pet. "There's Nibbles!"

Kirsty looked where Rachel was pointing and saw an orange and white hamster sitting on a cushion. She stepped a little closer, to get a better look at him.

"That isn't Nibbles," she told Rachel.
"Which means it must be…"

But before she could say another
word, the hamster twitched its little nose
and a bright shower of glittering red
sparkles swirled around it. When the
fairy dust cleared the
girls could see
a transparent
plastic tube,
spiralling down
from the sofa
to the carpet.

Immediately,
the hamster
jumped happily
into the tube and
started scampering
down through the spiral.

Kirsty laughed. "No," she said, "that's definitely not Nibbles. It absolutely has to be the magic hamster!"

Rachel smiled as the magical pet scurried busily down through the spiral it had conjured. "I wonder if Harriet the Hamster Fairy knows her pet is here," she said excitedly.

Before Kirsty could reply, both girls heard a breathless voice cry, "Wheee!" behind them. They turned, just in time to see a big black cloud of soot billowing out from the fireplace. As the coal-dust settled, Kirsty and Rachel grinned in delight. For there on the hearth, covered from head to toe in soot, was a tiny fairy!

Twinkle, Twinkle Little Hamster

The fairy sneezed three times, blinked, and then waved a sooty wand over herself. A bright stream of red sparkles shot out of the wand, whizzed around her and the soot disappeared in an instant. "That's better," she said cheerfully, and gave the girls a huge smile. "Hello, again!"

Now that she was free of soot, the
girls could see that Harriet the Hamster
Fairy was wearing a light blue dress,
tied with a darker blue sash. She wore
sparkly red shoes, and a glittery red
flower hung on a chain round her
neck, while another decorated the blue
Alice band in her short blonde hair.

"Hello, Harriet," Kirsty said, smiling at the little fairy. "We were just wondering if you were nearby."

"And here I am," Harriet said, smiling back. "I had a feeling that Twinkle, my pet, was somewhere around here."

"She is," Rachel said eagerly, "but there are three goblins too! We last saw them heading upstairs."

"Horrid things," Harriet said, fluttering up into the air, "but I'm glad Twinkle's here. Where is she?"

"She's just about to come out of that spiral tube," Kirsty said, pointing it out with a grin.

"Any second…now!"

Right on cue, Twinkle emerged. As soon as she saw Harriet, the hamster shrank to fairy pet size and scampered joyfully up into the air. Rachel and Kirsty watched in delight as the tiny magic hamster scurried towards her fairy mistress.

"Just what I was looking for!" came a gloating, goblin voice.

Rachel and Kirsty spun around in alarm to see a goblin pop up from behind the sofa with a horrible smirk on his face!

The goblin vaulted swiftly over the sofa, grabbed the tiny pet out of the air, and then rushed out of the lounge and up the stairs.

"Oh, no!" Rachel cried. "That goblin must have sneaked back downstairs looking for Twinkle. And now he's got her!"

"Quick, let's fly after him!"
Harriet suggested, waving
her wand and turning
both girls into fairies.
She zoomed out of
the door, leaving
glittering red fairy
dust shimmering
in the air behind
her, as Kirsty
and Rachel
followed using
their delicate,
shining wings.

As the three friends
flew upstairs, they
could see the goblins
standing on the next flight of
stairs that led to the upper storeys

of the house. But when they saw
fairies coming towards them,
the goblins turned and fled
to the second floor.
"Keep going!"
Harriet urged,
beating her wings
even faster as she
zoomed ahead.
"Let's hide in
here!" the girls
heard a goblin
shout, as they
reached the top of
the second flight
of stairs. They were
just in time to see
a goblin disappearing
through a doorway.

"That's Jamie's bedroom," Kirsty whispered, coming to a stop. "And it's not very big. There can't be too many hiding places in there."

"If we're girls again, it'll be easier for us to take Twinkle from the goblins," Rachel pointed out. "Could you magic us back, please, Harriet?"

"Of course," Harriet said. She waved her wand again, and sparkling red fairy dust tumbled all over Kirsty and Rachel. "There," she said, as the fairy dust worked its magic and the girls quickly grew back to their normal size.

"Now, let's go hamster hunting!"

Rachel and Kirsty crept into Jamie's
bedroom, with Harriet hovering behind
them. There was a bed, a wardrobe,
a chest of drawers and a large toybox,
but no goblins in sight.

Rachel headed straight
for the toybox and
lifted the lid. But
there was no
goblin inside,
just a collection
of Jamie's
plastic dinosaurs,
toy cars and some
colourful rubber snakes.

Kirsty tiptoed over to the bed and
checked under the lumpy duvet, but she
didn't find a goblin underneath.

Suddenly, Harriet started fluttering around excitedly, pointing to one of the long curtains that framed the window.

The girls crept forwards to have
a closer look, and grinned at each other
excitedly; there was a distinctly
goblin-shaped bump behind the curtain!

Hamster Hide and Seek!

Kirsty and Rachel looked at each other, both wondering what to do. Then Kirsty had an idea. She put her finger to her lips, warning the others to keep quiet. She wasn't sure if the goblin behind the curtain was the one with Twinkle or not, but if he did have the magic hamster, she wanted to catch him off guard.

If she could make him jump, she hoped
the goblin would loosen his grip on
Twinkle, who could then leap free!

Kirsty crept up to the curtain as
quietly as she could. Then, with a sharp
jab of her finger, she poked the curtain
right where she guessed the goblin's
tummy would be.

"Ow!" came a surprised shout.

"Caught you!"
Kirsty cried,
quickly tugging
the curtain
aside. "Now
give Twinkle
back!"

But the goblin
behind the curtain
was empty-handed.

He dodged past Kirsty and ran straight
out of the bedroom.

"So that's one goblin…" Harriet
mused. "Now, where
are the other two?"

But even as
Harriet spoke,
Rachel had
spotted a
pair of green
goblin feet
sticking out from
under the bed. She
tiptoed back to the toybox and pulled
out one of Jamie's rubber snakes. Then
she winked at Kirsty and Harriet, and
said in a loud voice, "Ooh! I think
I just saw a snake! Do the Coopers
have a pet snake too, Kirsty?"

"No," Kirsty said, guessing at Rachel's plan. "It must be a wild one. Look, there it goes, slithering under Jamie's bed! I wonder if it's poisonous..."

Trying her hardest not to giggle, Rachel pushed the rubber snake under Jamie's bed and made a loud hissing noise. Grinning cheekily, Harriet flung some red fairy dust after it, and the snake began wriggling further under the bed all by itself!

With a squeal of
alarm, the goblin
scrambled out
from his hiding
place and
rushed out of
the room. But
he wasn't holding
Twinkle either.

"That's two
goblins," sighed Harriet.
"Where could the third one be?"

Just then, the girls heard a nervous
laugh coming from inside the wardrobe.
They guessed that the third goblin must
be hiding inside it, and since the other
two didn't have Harriet's magic
hamster, this one must be the goblin
who had snatched Twinkle!

Kirsty and Rachel stood either side of the wardrobe, holding one door handle each. "One…two…three!" Rachel mouthed, then they flung open the wardrobe doors at the same time.

Kirsty's heart was pounding as she looked inside the wardrobe, ready to grab little Twinkle. But, to her dismay, there was nothing to see except lots of clothes hanging up. Had they misheard? Was the goblin somewhere else?

But sharp-eyed Harriet was pointing at something in the wardrobe and the girls saw that, there, sticking out between two of Jamie's superhero costumes, was a pointed green nose! The goblin was in the wardrobe, he was just well hidden.

Rachel spotted a Native American feathered headdress on the top shelf of the wardrobe and that gave her an idea. Kirsty and Harriet watched curiously as Rachel mimed pulling out a feather and using it to tickle the goblin's feet.

Harriet had to put a hand over her mouth to stop herself laughing at the idea. Nodding excitedly, she waved her wand over the headdress. A large red feather immediately glimmered with a sparkly light, and then leapt nimbly out of its place. The feather shot down towards the goblin's toes, where it began to tickle them all over!

"Ooh! Ahh! Ooh, stop that!" the goblin giggled, hopping from one foot to another. "Ooh! Ha ha! Stop it! Hee hee!"

The feather went on tickling away, until the goblin was breathless with laughter. Finally, he could stand it no more. "Stop!" he roared, between laughs. "Stop!"

"Not until you give us Twinkle!" Rachel and Kirsty chorused firmly.

Nibbles is Nowhere

The goblin's hands appeared through the clothes at once, with a tiny, fairy pet-sized Twinkle sitting in his cupped palms. "Here – take it! Take it!" the goblin urged. "Just stop the tickling!"

Harriet flew over and scooped up Twinkle. She dropped a kiss on the hamster's little head, then waved her

wand in the direction of the goblin's
feet. Sparkling red fairy dust swirled
around the feather, which glowed
brightly once more and leapt back into
its place in Jamie's headdress.

The goblin jumped out of the
wardrobe and bolted through the
bedroom door. "It's not fair, they were
tickling me," the girls heard him moan
to the other goblins.

Rachel and Kirsty
smiled at one
another, then
petted cute little
Twinkle. That
was one hamster
safe, at least!

"Now we just
have to find Nibbles,"
Rachel said. "I wonder
where he could have got to."

Twinkle was already twitching
her delicate nose and looking up at
Harriet in a meaningful way. The
fairy paid close attention, then
nodded at her pet. "Twinkle says
she senses that Nibbles is somewhere
up above us in the house," she told
Rachel and Kirsty.

"In the attic?" Kirsty said. "Wow, he's climbed a long way today!"

"Come on, let's find him right away," Rachel said, "before he goes off on another adventure!"

Kirsty, Rachel and Harriet all rushed up the last staircase to the attic door. But as soon as they stepped into the attic itself, all three of them gasped.

"Oh, no!" Kirsty cried, looking around. The small room was absolutely stuffed full of boxes and suitcases, old furniture, wooden trunks, dusty photo albums and trinkets, dimly lit by the daylight that streamed in through a tiny round window. "How are we ever going to find Nibbles in this lot?"

Luckily, Twinkle seemed to know exactly where Nibbles was. She was already scampering through the air towards a stack of travel souvenirs. Rachel could see carved wooden masks, a rather moth-eaten silk parasol, a jewellery box piled high with strings of beads, and even an old

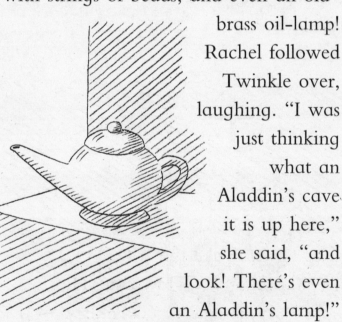

brass oil-lamp! Rachel followed Twinkle over, laughing. "I was just thinking what an Aladdin's cave it is up here," she said, "and look! There's even an Aladdin's lamp!"

Twinkle seemed interested in the lamp too. She pushed at it with her nose, then looked up at Harriet, her little black eyes bright with interest.

Rachel carefully lifted the lid of the lamp and everyone peeped inside curiously. There, curled up fast asleep, was Nibbles!

"Oh, look!" Rachel said, hurriedly dropping her voice to a whisper so as not to wake the sleeping hamster. "How cute. He's worn out after all his adventures!"

Kirsty gently scooped the sleepy
hamster out of the lamp, feeling very
relieved. Now all they had to do was
put Nibbles back in his cage with some
fresh food, and clean up the lounge.
Then everything would be exactly as it
should be once more.

But just as they were heading towards the door, Kirsty and Rachel heard the unmistakeable sound of goblin footsteps pounding up the attic stairs. The girls looked around quickly for some means of escape, but there was only one door and the tiny window. The goblins were coming, and the friends were trapped!

"Quick, Harriet!" Rachel cried. "Fly out of the window and take Twinkle home to Fairyland before those goblins can get their hands on her again."

"Yes," Kirsty agreed eagerly. "The goblins won't bother hanging around here once they know you and Twinkle have gone."

Harriet nodded, clutching her pet protectively. "OK, girls. Thank you both for all your help," she added, zooming over to the window. Then she stopped on the windowsill, as if she'd just remembered something. "But before I go, I'd better tidy up the mess downstairs."

Her wand was a bright blur in the air as Harriet waved it in a complicated pattern, sending glittering red fairy dust spiralling out of the door. "There!" she said, sounding pleased with herself.

"And thank you again, girls," she added, hugging them goodbye. "You've both been brilliant!"

"Goodbye Harriet. Goodbye Twinkle," Rachel and Kirsty said quickly, because the goblin footsteps were growing nearer by the second!

Harriet fluttered out through the open window, just as the three goblins clattered into the attic.

"After that fairy!" the first goblin shouted, seeing the last traces of fairy magic glimmering round the window.

"She's outside. Quick, let's follow her," the second one shouted, turning around so fast that he bumped straight into the third goblin.

"Hey! Watch where you're going!" snapped the third goblin, turning to hurry back down the attic stairs.

"Well, it's your fault that the hamster got away," Kirsty and Rachel heard one of the other goblins telling him as they all stomped away.

"My fault! How do you work that out?" came the indignant reply, drifting faintly up the stairs.

The goblins were soon out of earshot, so Rachel and Kirsty ran over to the attic window to see if they could spot them in the garden. Moments later, they saw the three goblins appear outside, bickering noisily about which way Harriet had gone.

A sparrow suddenly flew across the garden, and one of the goblins pointed excitedly at it. "There's the fairy!" he shouted. And the silly goblins chased eagerly after the sparrow as it darted over the back fence and into the meadow behind the Coopers' garden.

Meanwhile, on Kirsty's hand, Nibbles
opened his eyes and
gazed around as if
he was surprised to
find himself there.

"Hello, Nibbles,"
Kirsty said, stroking
him. "Let's get you something to eat.
What an adventure you've had!"

The girls headed back downstairs
and saw that Harriet had worked her
wonderful fairy magic, as promised;
the lounge was spotless.

"Wow!" said Rachel, with a grin.
"You'd never guess that this room was
full of wood shavings and hamster toys
just a few minutes ago!"

Kirsty put Nibbles back into his
cage and couldn't help smiling.

Harriet hadn't just taken care of the messy lounge, she'd also magically filled up Nibbles' bowl with a large helping of sunflower seeds! "His favourite food," Kirsty said, watching the hamster tuck in hungrily. "Clever Harriet!"

Kirsty carefully shut the cage door and looked at the happy little hamster for a few moments. "You know, I think I'll take Nibbles back to my house with us," she said. "Just so that we know for sure he's safe from any goblin mischief."

"Good idea," Rachel said. "Then Nibbles will get a little holiday, too."

Kirsty wrote a note
to Jamie, telling him
where Nibbles was,
and left it on the
table in the lounge.
Then she carefully
carried the hamster
cage over to the door.

"Phew," Rachel sighed, as she and
Kirsty left the Coopers' house. "That was
a busy morning!" She smiled at her friend.
"What could possibly happen tomorrow?"

Kirsty grinned. "I don't know," she
replied happily. "But I can't wait to
find out!"

Win Rainbow Magic Goodies!

There are lots of Rainbow Magic fairies, and we want to know which one is your favourite! Send us a picture of her and tell us in thirty words why she is your favourite and why you like Rainbow Magic books. Each month we will put the entries into a draw and select one winner to receive a Rainbow Magic Sparkly T-shirt and Goody Bag!

Send your entry on a postcard to Rainbow Magic Competition, Orchard Books, 338 Euston Road, London NW1 3BH.
Australian readers should email: childrens.books@hachette.com.au
New Zealand readers should write to Rainbow Magic Competition, 4 Whetu Place, Mairangi Bay, Auckland NZ.
Don't forget to include your name and address.
Only one entry per child.

Good luck!

RAINBOW magic ®

The Pet Keeper Fairies

Harriet the Hamster Fairy has got her
pet back. Now Rachel and Kirsty
must help

Molly the Goldfish Fairy

Gnome, Sweet Gnome

"Slow down, Dad," Kirsty Tate called. "You're leaving us behind!"

"Sorry," Mr Tate stopped and waited for Kirsty, Rachel and Mrs Tate to catch up. "I'm feeling hungry, and you know how good the Wainwrights' barbecues always are. In fact..." He sniffed the air. "I think I can smell the food cooking from here!"

"We're still two streets away!" Kirsty said, grinning and shaking her head at her best friend Rachel who burst out laughing.

Mr and Mrs Tate walked on and the girls followed.

"We'll have a good time at the barbecue," Kirsty said, smiling at Rachel who was staying with her for the holidays. "The Wainwrights have got a huge garden. It's lovely."

"Great!" Rachel said eagerly. Then she lowered her voice. "Don't forget, we must look out for fairy pets!"

Kirsty nodded. "The fairies are depending on us," she whispered.

Rachel and Kirsty had never told anyone their very special secret. They had become friends with the fairies and now, whenever their magical friends were in trouble, the girs always tried to help...

Have you checked out the

RAINBOW
magic®

website at:

www.rainbowmagic.co.uk